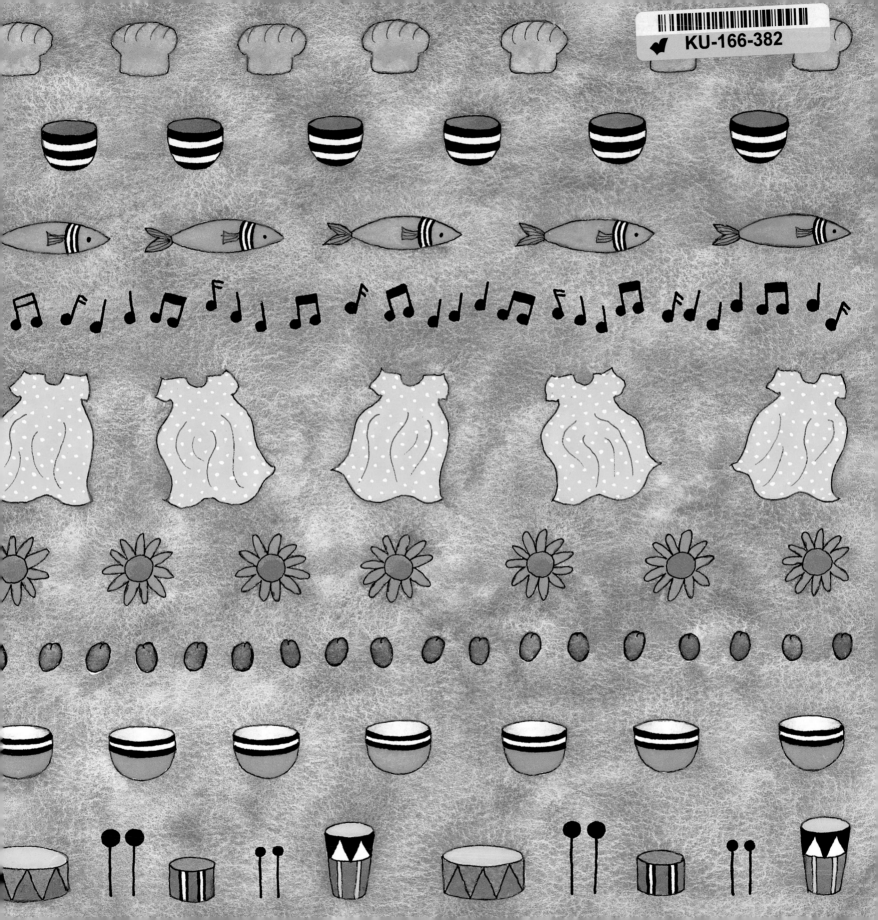

BEAR'S BUSY FAMILY

Written by Stella Blackstone
Illustrated by Debbie Harter

BAREFOOT BOOKS
BATH

Smell the bread
my grandma bakes

Touch the bowls
my grandpa makes

Taste the fish
my uncle brings

See the dress
my mummy sews

**Smell the flowers
my daddy grows**

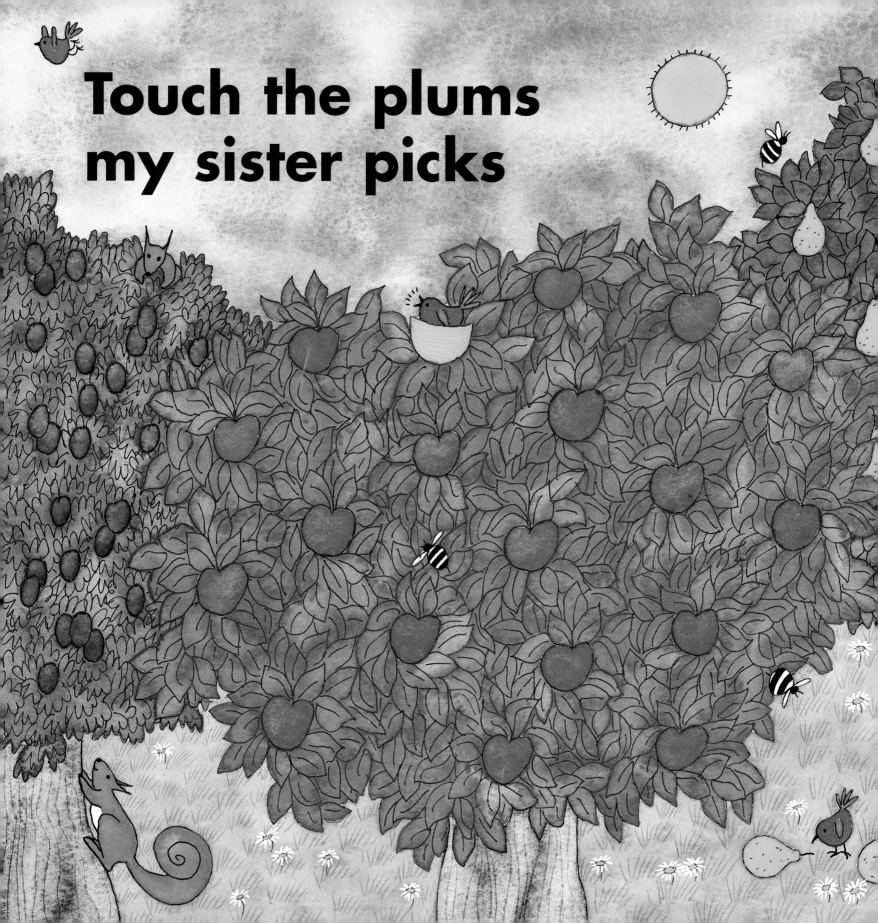

Touch the plums
my sister picks

Taste the bowl
my brother licks

See the feast for baby's birthday!

My Family Tree

grandma

daddy

baby

mummy

sister

brother

me

grandpa

uncle

auntie

cousins

For Mo, Kirsten, Matthew, Alice and Chloë — D.H.
For the Luecks, who are a very busy family — S.B.

Barefoot Beginners
an imprint of
Barefoot Books
PO Box 95
Kingswood
Bristol
BS30 5BH

Graphic design by Amesbury Grzelinski Ltd., Bath
Colour separation by Grafiscan, Verona
Printed and bound in Singapore by Tien Wah Press (Pte) Ltd.

This book was typeset in Futura and illustrated in watercolour,
pen and ink and crayon on thick watercolour paper

This book has been printed on 100% acid-free paper

Hardback ISBN 1 902283 89 9
Paperback ISBN 1 902283 91 0

British Cataloguing-in-Publication Data: a catalogue record for this
book is available from the British Library

1 3 5 7 9 8 6 4 2

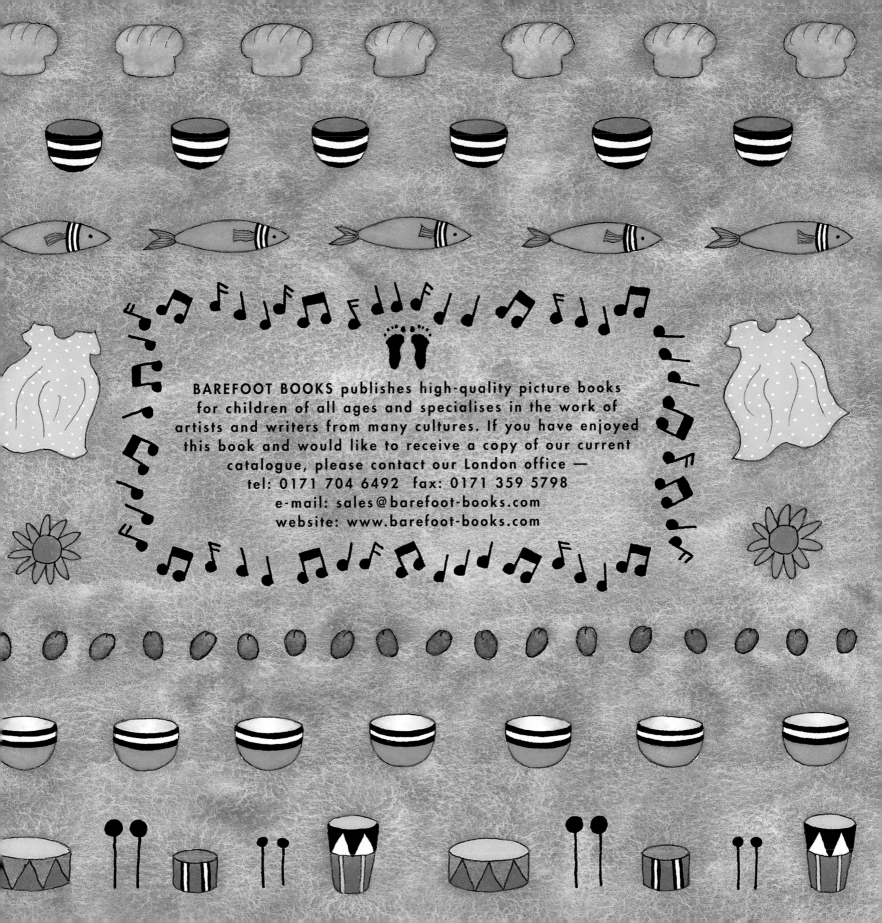

BAREFOOT BOOKS publishes high-quality picture books for children of all ages and specialises in the work of artists and writers from many cultures. If you have enjoyed this book and would like to receive a copy of our current catalogue, please contact our London office —
tel: 0171 704 6492 fax: 0171 359 5798
e-mail: sales@barefoot-books.com
website: www.barefoot-books.com